Paloma and the Dust Devil

AT THE BALLOON FESTIVAL

BY MARCY HELLER
ILLUSTRATED BY NANCY POES

AZRO PRESS • 2010

Paloma and the Dust Devil at the Balloon Festival
A magical balloon ride that carries Paloma
back in time in the Land of Enchantment.
For ages 4 to 10
Grades K - 6

ISBN 978-1-920115-19-8
Library of Congress Control Number: 2010927269

PMB 342 • 1704 Llano St B
Santa Fe, New Mexico 87505
www.azropress.com

Book designed by Marcy Heller
Display fonts: Monotype Corsiva and Goudy Old Style Italic
Text font & size: Goudy Old Style 14 point

Illustrations by Nancy Poes
Gouache on illustration board
www.nancypoes.com

Manufactured by Friesens Corporation
Manufactured in Altona, MB, Canada in June, 2010
Job # 56008

Author's dedication
To my ever-supportive husband, Brian McPartlon

Artist's dedication
To my beloved grandson, Leo George Shilling

Today is a special day. Paloma wakes up very, *very* early. She is so excited! Today her papa Hector promised to take her for a ride in a hot air balloon. Every fall their city hosts a gigantic balloon festival, and balloons come from all over the world. This is the first year Papa said she is old enough to ride in a balloon. Papa's father, *abuelo* Rafael, flew balloons too, and he gave Papa lots of rides.

Sometimes Mama says, with a very serious face, "I *know* I flew around the front yard all by myself when I was six years old." Paloma likes to dream that she is an astronaut. She dreams she flies around the whole world and out into the stars, not just around the front yard!

Papa's friend Gilbert lives in a nearby Pueblo. When he was in the army, Gilbert learned to fly hot air balloons for Uncle Sam, whoever that is. Paloma never met any uncles belonging to Gilbert. She had met his mother, his three sisters, a lot of nieces and nephews, and one aunt. But no uncle.

Today Gilbert will fly a balloon for one of the banks in town. He will give his first ride to Paloma and Papa.

Papa pokes his head in Paloma's bedroom door.

"I see you are all ready! Let's go get some breakfast burritos and then fly! We'll catch the wind!"

When they get to the balloon park, the sun still isn't up! Paloma has never been up this early, not even on Christmas morning.

They find Gilbert and his balloon in space 5C, right in the middle of the rows and rows of balloons. All around his balloon, his crew is checking lines. They blow air from a big fan into the balloon to start filling it up. Next they light a big propane burner that heats more air to fill the balloon completely. The hot air helps the balloon fly, because the hot air is lighter than the cooler, heavier air in the sky.

Paloma watches as the first row of balloons takes off. Then the second row, and then the third row. It's almost Gilbert's turn.

"Paloma! Let's go, *m'hijita*!" Papa lifts her into the big basket that is tied to the balloon. "We're all ready!"

Gilbert waits for the field official to give the signal to go, then he checks the propane burner one last time and calls to his crew, "Let 'er go!"

Up, up, up go Paloma, Papa, and Gilbert in the balloon.

"Paloma, I want to remind you about the rules we talked about last night," Gilbert says seriously. "Keep your arms inside the basket. Keep your knees bent in case we hit a bump in the air."

"A bump in the air? How does a bump get in the air, Gilbert?"

"The air travels in different layers. Sometimes one layer travels west while the layer right below it is going east! So your pilot, me, Gilbert, has to stay alert! No more questions, please!"

Paloma peeks carefully over the side of the basket. OOHH! The ground is getting farther and farther away. She looks to the side. They are surrounded by lots of other balloons. The balloons look so graceful as they float slowly up and away. As the wind catches them, they begin to drift away from each other.

Paloma closes her eyes and listens to the hissing of the burner. Suddenly everything becomes very quiet. Paloma opens her eyes. She sees that Gilbert has stopped burning the propane and they are way high up.

Papa squeezes her shoulders from behind and whispers, "Look, down there! You can see the river!"

Paloma lets out a big breath and realizes she has been holding it.

"Wow! We are so high up, Papa!"

"Yes, are you scared?"

Paloma looks at Gilbert, who is looking down river, and feels Papa's hands on her shoulders.

"No, I'm fine!"

On and on they fly. Paloma watches as the land and the river unroll below them. She can see so much from up here—there's the big Cotton Madera Mall. And the cars look like bugs zipping around! She sees horses in some of the old pastures that still lie near the river. One horse is white; it is running fast in a big circle. And there is an old barn that has little dots in front of it. Paloma thinks the dots must be chickens, because they scurry back and forth.

Paloma looks up to see the sky above them. All she can see is the big colorful balloon envelope that flaps gently above her. Wait a minute—what's that brown thing way off in the sky?

Paloma squints to see the brown thing more clearly, but suddenly the balloon bounces in the air. Papa's hands tighten on her shoulders, and Gilbert mutters something quietly to Papa.

"What is that, Gilbert? It's not a tornado, is it?"

"I think it might be a big dust devil that went really high up. Hold on, Paloma, I think we might be in for a bumpy ride!"

Paloma watches as the world spins around them once, twice, then three times.

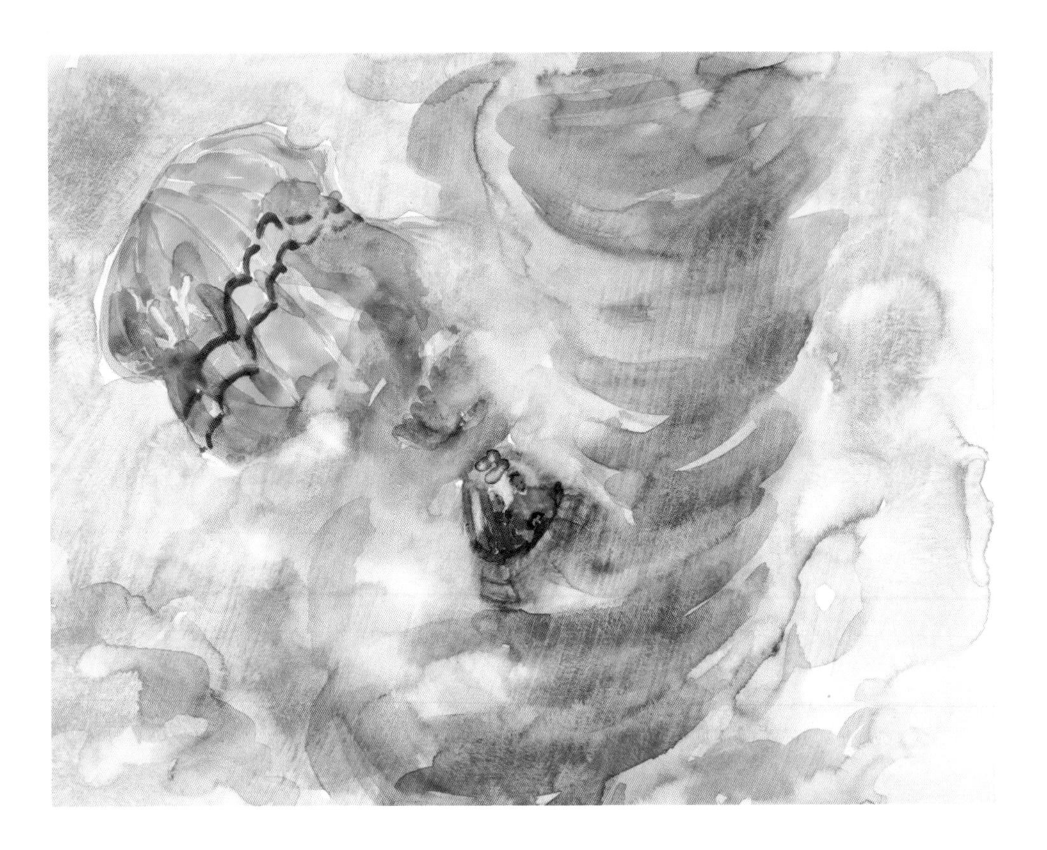

The third time around Paloma sees the brown thing. It looks like a big dusty funnel. It looks a lot closer than it did a minute ago.

The loose lines that hang from the sides of the basket begin to flap. The sky around them becomes very dusty. Paloma closes her eyes.

"Hector, help me bring this balloon down on the far side of the river. This dust devil is pushing us that way, and we want to get to its outer edges as fast as we can."

Gilbert and Papa begin to work the lines that let air out of the balloon. They are right inside the dust devil now, and it makes a strange wailing sound around their basket.

"*Whooooooooooooooooooooooooooooooo!*"

"Slowly, now."

"Whoa-hold on!"

Paloma peeks over the side of the basket. She glimpses the ground below them coming up fast.

"Paloma, hold on tight to the edge of the basket. Remember, keep your knees bent!"

Paloma bends her knees and takes a deep breath. Papa's hands are around her tummy now, holding her so tightly she can hardly take another breath.

BAM! The basket lurches sideways as it drags across a field. Then it comes back upright.

"Quick, Hector! Jump out and tether us to that tree! I turned off the propane burner. I will let the air out. Then we can wait for the crew to come get us."

Gilbert pulls harder on the lines. The envelope of the balloon collapses with a big POOF. The dust devil still pushes dust all around them. Then it suddenly pulls back and whooshes away. Paloma rubs the dust out of her eyes. She sees the brown spinning dust devil fly off toward the mesa. Then she looks over the edge of the basket.

What is that? A big brown horse is trotting over to them, ears held high. Papa finishes tying the line to the tree. He comes back and lifts Paloma out of the basket.

Gilbert holds his crew radio way out in front of him. He looks confused.

"Hector, I can't get any reception! Nothing! Not even a squawk!"

"Halloooo! Are you okay?"

Paloma turns around and sees a small woman running toward them. She looks different. She is wearing a long skirt and some kind of funny hat.

"Shoo! No apples today!" she scolds the horse. The horse shakes his head and follows the woman anyway.

Paloma takes a deep breath and rubs her eyes again. When she opens them, the woman is in front of her. She stops and looks slowly at Paloma, from head to toe and then back up to her head.

Paloma wipes her hand over her forehead, and it comes away with a little blood on it. Suddenly, Paloma feels dizzy. The woman catches her as she totters forward. Papa stoops down. He uses his bandanna to pat Paloma's head gently.

"It doesn't look serious, but let's get her to the house," says the woman. "My name is Aleta. A drink of water and a little rest will fix everything, I'm sure."

Paloma hears Papa whisper to her as he lifts her into his arms, "Aleta was the name of my *abuela's* mama. *Abuela* always said her mama was the mother who had wings. Aleta loved birds more than anything. She lived out here somewhere on the west side."

Aleta moves quickly despite her long skirts. Paloma closes her eyes again and bounces gently in Papa's arms as he strides along behind the woman. When Paloma opens her eyes next, she is lying on a *banco* in a smoky-smelling kitchen. Papa sits next to her on a stool, holding her hand.

"Ah, there you are! Let's drink some water now, Paloma!"
As Paloma sips from a tin cup, she looks around curiously. There is a kiva fireplace in the corner, just like in their family room at home. But there is no TV. On the other side of the kiva is a big wooden box. Soft scratching noises come from the box. At the other end of the room is a big iron stove. Paloma knows it is a stove, because Aleta is stirring a pot that sits on top of it, and a good smell rises from the pot. Next to the stove is a rickety little table. There is a window above it.

Just then, the door opens. A big man comes in and heads for a corner of the room.

"Ah *bueno*, I smell the *frijoles*!" he says to Aleta as he washes and wipes his hands.

Aleta says, "Severino, we have visitors."

Paloma hears Papa gasp. He turns a shade of gray that Paloma has never seen before.

Aleta looks hard at Papa. Papa looks hard at Aleta. Then he gulps and asks in a little voice, "Excuse me, please, but what is your family name?"

The big man looks at Papa and says in a deep voice, "Gonzales."

Paloma cries out, "Papa, that is our name too!"

"Sssssshhh now, Paloma. Señor, we have come to your rancho in a hot air balloon. We landed in your pasture. I am so sorry; we will pay you for any damages."

"A hot air balloon? I have never seen one!" Severino runs out the door toward the pasture.

Aleta turns to Paloma and Hector. "He does not mean to be rude. He is just crazy for the sky! But I think something is going on here that I do not understand. Where do you come from? We have a quiet life here in the valley. Visitors don't usually fall out of the sky!"

Paloma's father swallows hard and says, "Aleta, I think we came from somewhere very far away. I think I am your great-grandson, brought here by that dust devil."

"What?" gasps Aleta.

"See your wedding photo on the wall? We have that same photo at home. It is the studio portrait of my great-grandparents, who were married in–"

"–Albuquerque," finishes Aleta. "Well, then, I'm not surprised you flew here. This family has always been full of people who want to fly. I love birds, and Severino dreams of flying like a bird. But how did you get here from the future?" She breathes heavily and sits down suddenly. Then she jumps up again.

"That makes our little Paloma here my great-GREAT grandaughter! *Bienvenidos*, welcome, *mi corazon*!" She rushes over to the banco, hugs Paloma, and kisses her on the cheek.

Paloma hugs Aleta back. When she looks over Aleta's shoulder, Paloma sees her father wipe a tear from his cheek.

"SQUAWK! GROK GROK GROK!" Loud croaking sounds come from the wooden box.

"Aleta, what is that noise?" Hector jumps to his feet.

Aleta goes over and slowly takes the cover off the box. There stand two gawky ravens. They start to flap their wings wildly. They are standing on a wooden dowel that goes through holes low in the sides of the box. Aleta picks up a nearby bowl and a wooden spoon.

"Hush now! Here is some food." She puts ground meat on the spoon and holds it in front of first one raven, then the other. Each time the raven snatches the food out of the spoon.

"Why do you keep young ravens in your house, Abuela?" asks Paloma.

"Well, *m'hijita*, their mother had too many babies. She pushed these two out of the nest because she could not take care of so many. Fortunately, I came along soon after they landed on the ground. They were croaking so sadly, and they were hungry! Now they are getting big and fat and soon can fly away!"

THE

"That's a wonderful story!" says Hector. "They're lucky they have you! I remember my grandmother told stories about you taking care of birds every spring." Hector's voice trails away; he looks very puzzled.

"What is it, Hector? I may call you Hector like your friend did out in the field, *sí?*"

"Of course! Our family also tells crazy stories about your husband, Severino Gonzales. Why, it is said that he could fly on his own just by wishing it!"

Paloma feels more and more confused. "What do you mean, Papa? How could anyone fly all by himself?"

A deep voice booms, "There are many strange and wonderful things in this world, *m'hijita*. Sometimes the weather can help; sometimes a certain phrase carries a power that could surprise you. Sometimes your dreams can come true, like your dream of flying through the stars."

Paloma swings her feet off the *banco* and sees the big man leaning in the window over the kitchen table. How does he know about her dreams?

"I was listening to you, Aleta, and also to Hector. I think what he says makes sense. The dust devil slipped through a crack in time to bring them to us. But we must help them get back to their own time."

"But I'm so tired," thinks Paloma as she yawns.

Her father walks over to her and says, "He is right, Paloma. We must get back to our own time. Let's go find Gilbert."

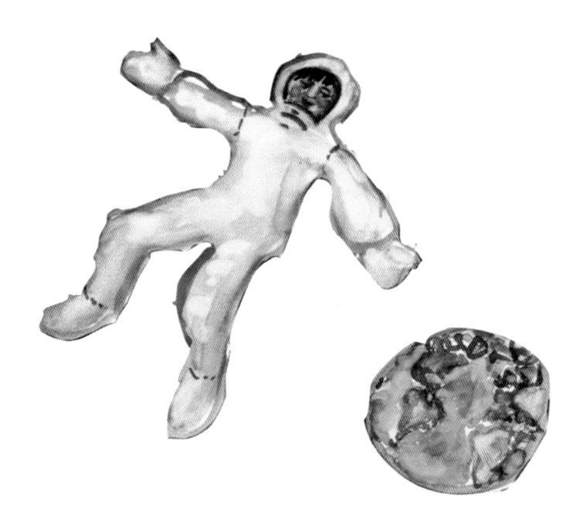

They all walk back out to the pasture. Hector talks to Gilbert quickly and quietly, and they begin to lay out the balloon on the soft grass. Severino helps and asks many questions.

Aleta gently brushes Paloma's hair back from her face and looks deeply into her eyes.

"Be a good girl, Paloma. Always follow your dreams. I am so happy to see you and to see that our family is doing well."

Paloma cries because she is tired and because she is very fond of this lady, even after such a short time.

"I think we're ready to inflate the balloon," says Gilbert. He asks Severino and Aleta to hold up the edges of the envelope to help inflate it with wind. Then he turns on the propane burner to inflate the balloon.

The wind begins to blow again. Hector lifts Paloma up so she can give a final hug, first to Aleta and then to Severino.

"Remember this, Paloma," whispers Severino in her ear. "The phrase 'catch the wind' holds some magic for you. Say it to yourself over and over as you fly back to your time. That will help you get there safely. And remember to look for a surprise from me."

"Thank you so much! I will never forget you!" Paloma tells Severino. She wants to ask about the surprise, but it's time to get into the basket. The balloon is full of warm air, so Gilbert calls to Severino and Aleta, "Okay, let 'er go!"

A sudden gust of wind sweeps the balloon up and away. Paloma peeks over the side and sees Severino and Aleta waving up at them. She waves back, then quickly grabs the side of the basket because it is swaying back and forth.

"Catch the wind, catch the wind, catch the wind," she whispers to herself. She shuts her eyes tightly. She feels dust hit her face.

"Gilbert, look to the west! That looks like the same big dust devil heading back our way!"

Paloma peeks out again and sees the brown funnel cloud coming toward them. "Catch the wind, catch the wind, catch the wind!" she shouts out loud this time. Paloma's father looks at her curiously and then yells, "Catch the wind, catch the wind, catch the wind!" right at the dust devil.

The dust devil wails back, "*WHOOOOOOOOOOOOOO!*"

Now they are in the cloud of stinging dust. Gilbert doesn't say anything, because he is busy adjusting the burner and looking all around. But Hector and Paloma still call out, together now, "Catch the wind!"

Suddenly they pass into clear air. The sky is blue and the wind is soft and quiet.

"Look, Gilbert!" shouts Hector. "There is the mall, and the highway, and all the houses...." He and Gilbert look at each other, then at Paloma.

"It worked!" shouts Paloma.

They drift eastward and soon catch up with a group of balloons flying south. Gilbert jumps as his radio squawks.

"Gilbert, there you are! Where in the world have you been?"

Gilbert winks at Paloma and presses the button on his radio. "We just took a little detour. Meet you downwind in about three miles."

Paloma and her father hug as Gilbert shakes his head and gives them both a big smile.

"I don't know how you two did that, but I think you do! Thanks for bringing us back!"

Gilbert guides the balloon slowly back toward the dusty earth. All around them, other balloons fill the sky as they drift toward a landing field. The crews follow them on the ground in the balloon crew trucks.

They all pack up their balloons carefully.

"How did your balloon get so dirty, Gilbert?" they ask.

"We went a little farther than usual," he replies. He puts his finger to his lips as he looks at Paloma and Hector. Paloma smiles back. She waves as she climbs into the truck with her father.

When Paloma gets back home, her mother comes to the door and gives her a big hug.

"How was your first balloon ride, Paloma?"

"Oh, it was the best flight ever, Mama!"

"Good! Now run upstairs and see if you can wash off some of that brown dust you're covered in!"

Paloma walks slowly upstairs to her room. Then she notices something in her back pocket. It's an envelope.

The ink is a faded brown, but she clearly sees the name Severino Gonzales in beautiful script in the left-hand corner. She sits down at her desk and opens the letter carefully. A dry chile pod falls out, full of seeds that rattle. She reads the letter.

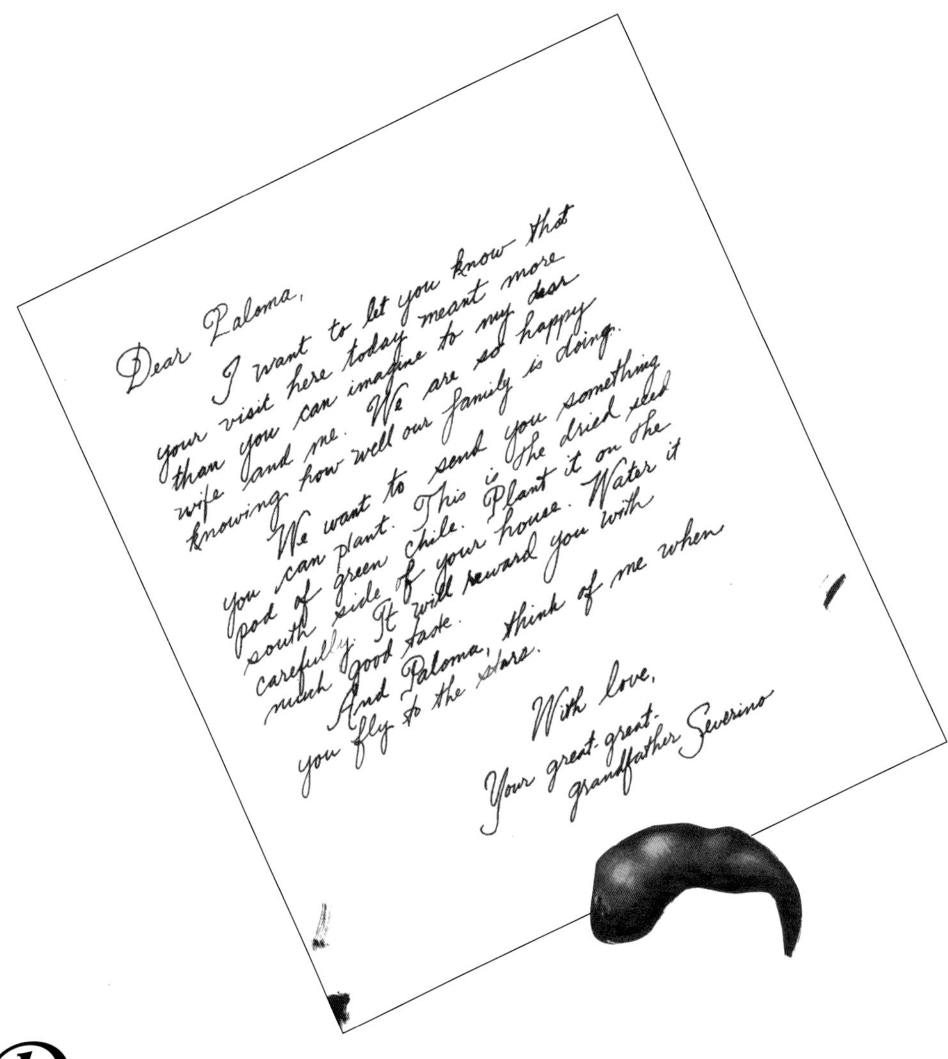

Dear Paloma,
I want to let you know that
your visit here today meant more
than you can imagine to my dear
wife and me. We are so happy
knowing how well our family is doing.
We want to send you something
you can plant. This is the dried seed
pod of green chile. Plant it on the
south side of your house. Water it
carefully. It will reward you with
much good taste.
And Paloma, think of me when
you fly to the stars.

With love,
Your great-great-
grandfather Severino

Dear Paloma,

I want to let you know that your visit here today meant more than you can imagine to my dear wife and me. We are so happy knowing how well our family is doing.

We want to send you something you can plant. This is the dried seed pod of a green chile. Plant the seeds on the south side of your house. Water them carefully. They will reward you with much good taste.

And Paloma, think of me when you fly to the stars.

With love,
Your great-great-grandfather
Severino

Author's Note,

Diagram of a Balloon,

A Brief History of Hot Air Ballooning,

and

Acknowledgments

Dear Reader,

I first wrote about an unusual and powerful dust devil in *Loco Dog and the Dust Devil in the Railyard* (Azro Press, 2008). In this new book the magical powers of the dust devil are transformed to impart time travel. I hope you enjoy Paloma's journey as much as I did!

When we are younger readers, we don't know what routes our lives will take. My life benefitted from two major influences. My mother was a librarian who brought home stacks of books every week for me to read. My father was a pilot who took aerial photographs for the U.S. Forest Service. He helped develop the field of research called remote sensing. The satellite images you can find today on the Internet are descended from the black-and-white photographs my father took using a camera mounted in the belly of an airplane. I got to spend many hours in an airplane with my father, from whom I acquired a love of flying.

Humanity has long dreamed of flying among the clouds and the stars. One story, which comes from Greek mythology, concerns a boy named Icarus. As old as this story is, it speaks to us still of man's yearning to fly. When Icarus and his father became captives on the island of Crete, his father made wings out of wax and feathers so they could escape.

"Don't fly too close to the sun or too near the water," he told Icarus before they strapped on their wings.

Icarus forgot what his father had said. He was having so much fun swooping around in the sky that he decided to fly higher to get a better view of the sun. The hot rays of the sun melted the wax, and all the feathers fell away. Icarus fell into the deep blue sea and was never seen again.

All flight involves risk because of a law of physics—gravity! But today airplanes enable us to travel many miles in a short time. Or, perhaps you would prefer a slower ride in a balloon, drifting silently on the breeze.

Keep reading!
Marcy Heller

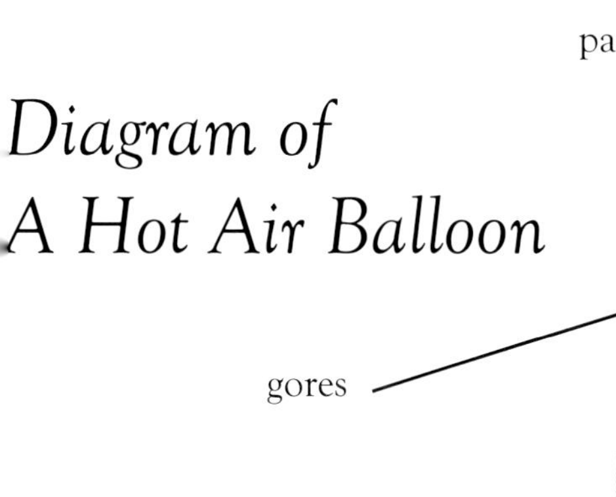

Diagram of A Hot Air Balloon

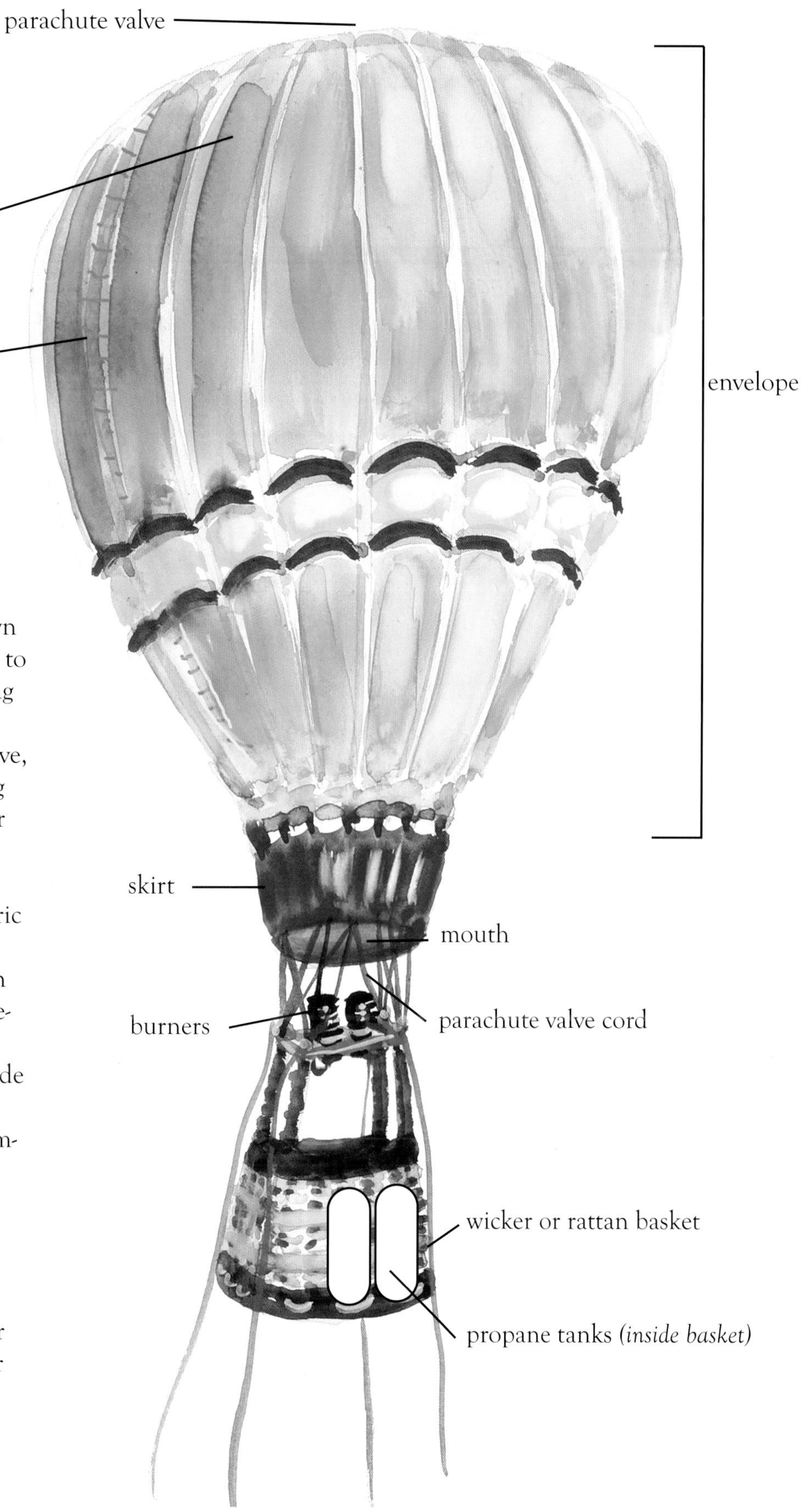

At the very top of the balloon is he parachute valve, which the pilot perates to bring a floating balloon lown to a lower altitude. The parahute valve is a circle cut out of the op of the fabric envelope. It is conrolled by a long cord that runs down hrough the middle of the envelope to he basket. If the pilot wants to bring he balloon down, he pulls on the ord. Pulling the cord opens the valve, etting hot air escape and decreasing he inner air temperature. As the air n the envelope cools, the balloon lows its climb.

The envelope is the balloon fabric either nylon or Dacron) that holds ir. Fabric gores and panels are sewn ogether to provide the balloon envepe with strength and structure.

The burner propels heat up inside he envelope.

The fuel tanks hold a highly compressed gas, propane, which flows hrough hoses to a heating coil. An ntake hose runs from the heating nit to the bottom of the propane anks, which are located inside the asket. The basket is made of wicker r rattan, which absorb shock better han a rigid material would.

A Brief History of Hot Air Ballooning

Hot air ballooning can be traced back more than 225 years. In 1782, two brothers in southern France began experimenting with steam, heated air, and balloons. Joseph and Etienne Montgolfier were sons of the wealthy owner of a paper factory. Joseph made a balloon from paper he got from the factory, then experimented with filling it with steam. He ended up with a big wet mess of paper!

Next his brother, Etienne, tried to make a paper bag rise into the air using hydrogen gas he made from iron filings and sulfuric acid. It did not float either. Then, Joseph made a taffeta envelope and filled it with hot air, releasing it to float around inside their house.

Now Joseph and Etienne were excited! They started preparing for the outdoor launch of a large balloon. On June 4, 1873, their hot air balloon took off from Annonay, France. The balloon had a volume of 800 cubic meters (about 1,046 cubic yards) and rose 1,000 meters (about 3,281 feet), travelling for 2 kilometers. The balloon was made of linen that was fireproofed with a coating of alum, and its segments were held together by buttons. The balloon was held over a burning fire to fill it with smoke. The brothers believed the blacker the smoke, the better the balloon would fly. They threw all kinds of things on the fire—even wet wool! They planned to call the dark smoke "Mongolfier gas." Later they learned that the cause of the balloon lift-off was the hot air, not the smoke.

The Montgolfier Brothers' first launch. *Library of Congress*, Prints and Photographs Division, [reproduction number, LC-DIG-ppmsca-02562]

When word of the Montgolfier brothers' success reached the capital of France, the brothers were invited to Versailles to demonstrate balloon flight to King Louis XVI; his queen, Marie Antoinette; and the entire French court. For that flight, the brothers decided to try something new, and on September 19, 1783, they added a duck, a sheep, and a rooster as the first living passengers in a hot air balloon.

Then on November 21, 1783, the Montgolfier brothers organized the first manned untethered flight. That balloon rose to 900 meters (more than half a mile) and traveled for 25 minutes to a landing 10 kilometers (more than 6 miles) away. On January 19, 1784, a Montgolfier hot air balloon carried seven passengers to 3,000 feet above Lyons.

In 1785, a French balloonist, Jean Pierre Blanchard, and his American co-pilot, John Jefferies, became the first to fly across the English Channel. Crossing the English Channel was considered the first hurdle in long-distance ballooning. On January 7, 1793, M. Blanchard became the first to fly a hot air balloon in North America, a launch witnessed by President George Washington. Blanchard carried the first piece of airmail—a passport given to him by President Washington.

As time went on, balloons were put to military use. After President Lincoln saw a balloon flight in 1861, he authorized the formation of the Balloon Corps. It used balloons to perform aerial reconnaissance of Confederate troops. The USS George Washington Parke Custis, a converted coal barge, became the first "aircraft carrier" as it towed and launched balloons from its deck. The Confederate army also tried to utilize balloons, but had only enough resources to assemble two—one of them made from donated silk dresses!

Much later, in the twentieth century, a man named Ed Yost founded a company to design and build hot air balloons for the United States Navy's Office of Naval Research. The Navy wanted balloons that could carry small loads short distances. Yost and his team expanded on the Montgolfier balloon, adding a propane burner system, new envelope materials, a new way to inflate the balloon, and many safety features. Yost's team also came up with the lightbulb, or teardrop, envelope shape that is common today.

By the early 1960s, the Navy had lost interest in hot air balloons, and Yost began selling them as sporting equipment. Other companies were formed as more and more people got involved in ballooning. Over the years, designers have continued to modify and elaborate on the designs of hot air balloons, developing new materials, safety features, and creative envelope shapes.

The balloon festival that Paloma attends in this book takes place in the small city of Albuquerque, New Mexico. The festival began in 1972 to help celebrate the 50th anniversary of the founding of radio station KOB. The radio manager asked Sid Cutter, the first person to own a hot air balloon in New Mexico, if he would fly his balloon as part of the celebration. Then the idea of a gathering of hot air balloons developed. Although 21 balloonists committed to attending, bad weather prevented all but 13 from arriving. On April 8, 1972, the balloons ascended from the parking lot of a local shopping center.

Things have changed a lot! Albuquerque's balloon festival has grown each year and now must limit attendance to 750 balloons. The city built a balloon fiesta park to accommodate the hundreds of balloons and thousands of people who come every year to ride or watch the balloons.

There are many balloon meets all over the country. If you can visit one, you too can further explore this marvelous sport.

Acknowledgments

Nancy and I owe many thanks to a lot of people who helped with this book. First and foremost, we greatly appreciate the support of our publisher, Gae Eisenhardt, of Azro Press here in Santa Fe.

Secondly, our loyal and tireless editor, Moya Melody, was invaluable in all the ways that an editor can be – persistent, stubborn and exacting! Thanks for being such a good editor and friend, Moya.

We were supported by the love of our families and by our many dog companions. Life was never dull around the studio where *Paloma* was written and painted.